EEK!
Stories to make you shriek™

For Beginning Readers
Ages 6-8

This series of spooky stories has been created especially for beginning readers—children in first and second grades who are developing their reading skills.

How do these books help children learn to read?

- Kids love creepy stories and these stories are true page-turners (but never too scary).
- The sentences are short.
- The words are simple and repeated often in the story.
- The type is large with lots of room between words and lines.
- Full-color pictures on every page act as visual "clues" to help children figure out the words on the page.

Once children have read one story, they'll be asking for more!

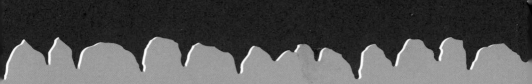

For my author buddies, Lorie Ann Grover and Sue Uhlig—J.H.

For Becky, Elizabeth, Helen, and Susan:
great artists and true friends—C.F.

Text copyright © 1999 by Joan Holub. Cover illustration copyright © 1999 by Joan Holub.
Interior illustrations copyright © 1999 by Cynthia Fisher. All rights reserved. Published by
Grosset & Dunlap, Inc., a member of Penguin Putnam Books for Young Readers, New York.
EEK! STORIES TO MAKE YOU SHRIEK is a trademark of The Putnam & Grosset
Group. GROSSET & DUNLAP is a trademark of Grosset & Dunlap, Inc. Published
simultaneously in Canada. Printed in the U.S.A.

Library of Congress Cataloging-in-Publication Data

Holub, Joan.
The spooky sleepover / by Joan Holub.
p.   cm. — (Eek! Stories to make you shriek)
Summary: While sleeping over at Emily's house, Jen and Emily tease Sara by telling scary
stories, but Sara ultimately has the last laugh.
[1. Sleepover—Fiction. 2. Storytelling—Fiction. 3. Horror stories.] I. Title. II. Series.
PZ7.H7427Sp   1999
[Fic]—dc21   98-49989
                                                                                                        CIP
ISBN 0-448-42043-0 (GB)   A B C D E F G H I J   AC

ISBN 0-448-42025-2 (pbk)   A B C D E F G H I J

Easy-to-Read

Ages 6-8

EEK!

Stories to make you shriek™

The Spooky Sleepover

By Joan Holub
Illustrated by Cynthia Fisher

Grosset & Dunlap • New York

Emily's Story

"Let's tell spooky stories," said Emily.

It was Friday night, and

Jen and Sara were sleeping over.

"No!" said Sara.

"We just watched that spooky video.

That is enough scary stuff for tonight."

Jen poked Sara and turned off
the light.

"Don't be such a fraidy-cat," she said.
Sara pulled her sleeping bag
up over her nose.
"Okay, but if I wake up screaming,
it will be your fault."

Emily went first.

She began her story in a spooky voice....

Knock! Knock!

It was a dark, dark night.

Three girls had a sleepover.

They ate pizza and painted their nails.

Then they watched a scary video.

But there was something very strange

about their video.

They were the stars of it!

The video showed them eating pizza

and painting their nails.

Then it showed them

turning on a scary video.

Could it be?

It was a video of <u>them</u>

at their sleepover!

The three girls were too scared to move.

So they kept watching.

In the video, a dark, dark shadow

was by the gate of the girls' house.

Knock! Knock!

"I am coming!" said the shadow.

And the gate opened.

Squeeeeek!

The dark, dark shadow

floated to their front door.

Knock! Knock!

"I am coming!" said the shadow.

And the door swung open.

Creeeek!

The dark, dark shadow
crept up the stairs.

Thump! Thump! Thump!

"I am coming!" said the shadow.

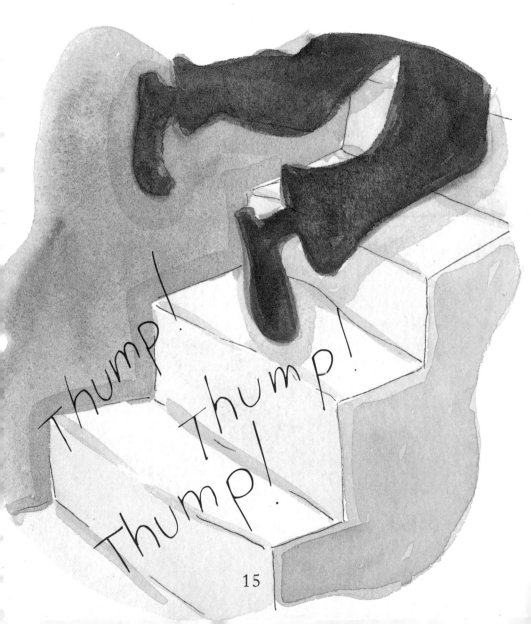

Thump!
Thump!
Thump!

Soon the girls in the video

heard a noise outside their door.

They screamed.

At the same time,

the girls watching the video

heard a noise outside <u>their</u> door.

They screamed, too.

The girls turned off the video.

But it was too late!

Knock! Knock!

They heard a spooky voice say,

"I am here!"

Just then, there really <u>was</u> a knock
on Emily's bedroom door.

Knock! Knock!

Emily, Jen, and Sara screamed. *Aaahh!*

18

Emily's mom came in,
holding a tray
of crackers and juice.
"What's wrong?" she asked.
"I just brought you snacks."

Jen's Story

"Oooh! Your story was scary!"

Jen told Emily.

"But I've got one that's even scarier!"

Sara jumped up and

turned on the light.

"No!" she said. "No more!"

But Emily turned the light back off.

"Don't be such a fraidy-cat,"

she teased.

Sara sighed and gave up.

Jen was quiet for a minute.

Then she began her story

in a creepy voice....

Snack Attack

There once was a greedy girl

who loved animal crackers.

Before she ate one, she would say,

"I'm gonna get you."

Then she would bite off its head,

its legs, and its tail.

And then she would gobble it up.

One day at school,

there was a new snack machine.

It had lots of yummy munchies.

But it had only one bag of

Creepy Critter Animal Crackers.

The girl had to have those crackers.

So she pushed ahead of a kid in line.

She put her money in the machine.

And she got the crackers.

But just as she was about to open

them, the bell rang.

So she stuffed the

bag in her pocket

and went to class.

In math class, the girl thought she heard

a strange noise coming from her pocket.

Crinkle, crackle.

It sounded like the bag was moving.

She listened again. Nothing.

During reading, she thought

she heard a weird voice.

"We're gonna get you!" it said.

"What?" she asked the boy next to her.

"I didn't say anything," he said.

Soon school was over.

By then, the girl was soooo hungry!

But she did not want to share

any crackers with her friends.

She decided she would

eat them when she got home.

The girl reached inside her pocket.

She felt the bag with her fingertips.

In one corner, it felt like

the bag had come open.

That's strange, thought the girl.

She had not opened it.

When she got home,

the girl ran to her room.

She could hardly wait

to eat those crackers.

She pulled the bag out of her pocket

and ripped it all the way open.

She stuck her hand in the bag.

And then the strangest

thing happened....

Something nibbled at the girl's fingers!

She pulled her hand out

and dropped the bag.

It was moving.

Crinkle, crackle.

The animal crackers were alive!

And they were crawling

out of the bag—one by one!

"We're gonna get you!" they said

in their tiny cracker voices.

Crinkle, crackle.

Just then, Jen poked a bag of animal

crackers that Emily was holding.

Crinkle, crackle.

Emily screamed and dropped the bag.

Jen giggled. "Got you!" she said.

Sara's Story

Sara peeked out from under

her sleeping bag.

"<u>Now</u> are we done with

the scary stuff?" she asked.

Emily shook her head.

"Nope," she said.

"Now it's your turn to tell

a spooky story.

That is, if you know any."

Sara thought it over.

"Weeeell, maybe one," she said.

"But it's too scary."

Now Emily and Jen looked excited.

"Oh, come on," said Emily.

"<u>We</u> aren't fraidy-cats."

Sara shrugged.

"Okay," she said.

"But don't say I didn't warn you."

Sara began her story in a scary voice....

Fraidy-Cat

Once, a girl went to a sleepover
with two friends.

She did not like scary things.

But the girl's friends made her
watch a spooky video.

Then her friends told scary stories.

So the girl decided to get even. How?

Well, there was something

the girl's friends

didn't know about her.

She had magic powers.

She could turn sleeping girls

into anything she wanted.

So that night at the sleepover,

the girl waited.

Soon her friends were asleep.

At the very stroke of midnight,

she crept over to them.

The girl pointed one finger

at each of her friends.

Her hair stood up straight.

A chilly breeze blew through the room.

The girl said a few magic words....

"Spooky, kooky, slimy slug—

icky, sticky, grimy bug."

Poof! No more friends.

Instead, there was a slimy slug
where one friend used to be.
And there was an icky roach
where the other friend used to be.

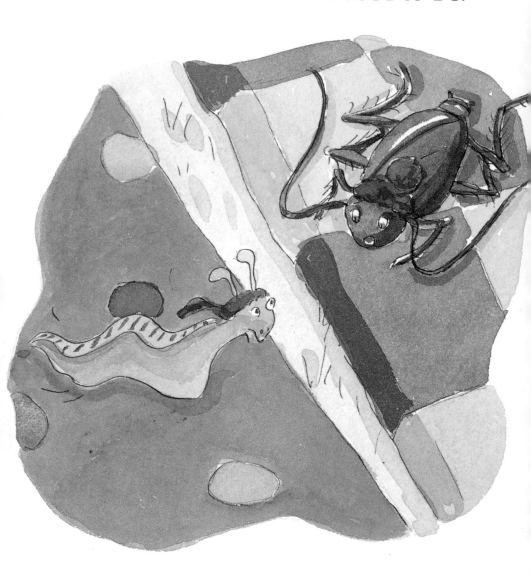

The girl scooped up

the slug and the roach.

She put them in a glass jar.

On Monday, she would take her

new pets to school for sharing time.

Sara smiled a spooky smile.

Emily and Jen stared at her

with big eyes.

"Your story's not true, right?"

Emily asked.

"You aren't really mad at us, right?"

Sara smiled another spooky smile.

"Come on," said Jen.

"Say it's not true,

or we'll never get to sleep!"

"Why?" Sara asked softly.

She pulled up her sleeping bag

and closed her eyes.

"What are you—fraidy-cats?"